Invincible: The Grave Robber

Invincible, Volume 1

Luke Pens

Published by LukePens, 2024.

INVINCIBLE:THE GRAVE ROBBER

First edition. December 5, 2024.

Copyright © 2024 Luke Pens.

ISBN: 979-8230149941

Written by Luke Pens.

Table of Contents

Dedicated to My little Anna who constantly assured me
i could be a good author

"In the darkest night, even the fiercest shadows must fade, for light will always find a way to break through."

Invincible: The grave Robber

Chapter 1: The gift

Samael elevated his fist in fury and brought it crashing down onto the table. He gazed intently into the eyes of everyone at the dinner table, as if penetrating right into their souls.
"What do you mean you sold them?!" he seethed at Lara.
"In my defense," Lara commenced, "I requested a couple of bucks, and you declined!"
She gulped a substantial amount of pickle juice and subsided deeper into her chair. Samael edged closer to her, causing her to squirm even further in her seat.
"I demand the particulars of this 'friend' you sold it to," he muttered under his breath, reiterating it two more times, progressively louder. Finally, Lara acquiesced with a nod.

Back at the McEwen's residence, where the sold item resided, Milly had just endured a significant altercation with her family at the dinner table. She fled into her room and slammed the door behind her. Her parents probably hadn't raised her correctly... probably.
A soft knock resonated at the door, followed by a series of urgent raps. Mr. McEwen rose and made his way to the door. He cautiously opened it and peered outside. There stood a heavily bearded man of medium stature, his gray eyes glimmering with a hint of silver in the darkness. Then, he flung the door wide and stepped inside.

"McEwen, I presume," the man—Samael—intoned in an oddly deep voice, gazing up at the towering Mr. McEwen, who stood at roughly 6'7".

"I am... who's inquiring?" McEwen replied.

"Could I have a word with Milly, your daughter?"

"Look, buddy, we're in the midst of a family dinner, and you appear to be at least 45."

"It's not what you think; she merely possesses a gift that my daughter bestowed upon her."

"You mean the bangle?"

"Is that what you call it?" Samael asked, raising an eyebrow. Before McEwen could respond, Samael had already brushed past him into the house, crossing paths with Milly and Mrs. McEwen, and ascending the stairs toward Milly's room. McEwen followed him, seething with anger, quickly catching up. He was about to open the door to the room when he was seized and flung across the upstairs hallway. McEwen was remarkably strong—so strong, in fact, that during his military service, he was nicknamed "Catapult" because rumors circulated that he could hurl a hand grenade up to 100 meters, and when ammunition ran low, he would wield his rifle like a bat; one strike from it could fracture ones cranium.

He then began advancing toward Samael on the ground, but a piercing scream from Milly's room halted him in his tracks. He attempted to open the door, only to find it locked from the inside. Summoning all his strength, he kicked the door open, shattering the lock.

Inside, Milly lay on the floor, and beside her was another girl with skin scalded, likely by acid or boiling water. As soon as the lights flickered on, she bolted through the window with astonishing speed. Samael pursued her, matching her velocity. The girl landed on her feet, breaking them but continuing to crawl at a frantic pace.

Samael landed softly, as if the ground were cushioned, rolled slightly, and resumed his chase. Mr. McEwen stood frozen in fear, beads of sweat trickling down his neck and back. He questioned his sanity, trying to dismiss the scene as a mere hallucination. Mrs. McEwen and Molly rushed to the scene, witnessing Milly on the floor. Mr. McEwen, still bewildered, turned to leave the room, only to find Samael behind him. He screamed, in the most manly voice possible, startling everyone, including Samael.

"It's no longer safe; they'll be back, and this time they're ready to kill. Please, let's go..." Samael pleaded as he finally had everyone's attention.

"You come into my house..." Mrs. McEwen began, advancing toward Samael. "Bamboozle around," she continued, "and now you want us to leave our home?"

"You don't know what you're up against..." Before Samael could finish, Mr. McEwen, now conscious, seized him by the collar and dragged him outside, shoving him far from the door. "Next time you try to set foot in my house, I will blow your brains out," he muttered angrily under his breath, slamming the door shut.

He headed back to Milly's room, and upon seeing him, she screamed, "Please don't kill me!"

"Honey, I wouldn't..." McEwen reassured her, inching closer, but she crawled further into the corner.

"Neil..." Mrs. McEwen started, apparently Neil was Mr. McEwen's first name. "Let us handle her for now. You look tired; get some rest."

Nile shrugged and walked downstairs to his bedroom. He sat on the bed, his mind racing and heartbeat pounding, but relaxed a few minutes later when Mrs. McEwen's hand grazed his shoulder, as if her touch absorbed all his worries.

"Are you alright, dear?" she asked.

"Yes, I'm well. How's Milly?"

"She's alright. The poor girl might have been hallucinating."

"I knew the lighter meant something; she probably was smoking."

"Maybe, but for now, she's fast asleep. Let's monitor her behavior when she wakes up."

"Sure," Neil replied in a deep, manly voice, trying to end the conversation. He tossed his shirt into the laundry basket and sank into bed, turning off the lamp.

Mrs. McEwen caressed his hair, and taking off her glasses, she joined him in bed, cuddling close. Neil pulled her even tighter, kissing her lightly on the cheek. He slid his heavy masculine arms beneath her nightdress, feeling her tummy gently. As he moved up to caress her nipples with the tip of his index finger, she took deep breaths. He tried to withdraw his hands, but she pulled them back, placing them atop her bosom.

Her right arm ventured to the lace of his sleeping pants, loosening them. When she felt his arousal, she gasped, as if surprised. She pushed him over so he lay on his back, then unbuttoned her nightdress, revealing her full, succulent breasts. Mounting him like one would a bike, she rubbed herself against the bulge in his pants, eliciting a soft, deep moan from him. She leaned in, kissing him softly, as if to absorb his moans. Then, she pressed her right nipple into his mouth, and he caressed it with his tongue in a circular motion, causing her to moan even louder.

Holding the back of his head, she pulled him closer, deepening the connection. He moved back, panting, then sat upright at the head of the bed. Grabbing her by the back of the neck, he drew her lips closer for another warm kiss. His right arm held her in place while his left explored her, gently pushing his fingers deep inside her, causing her to take a deep breath and moan simultaneously.

She responded by taking charge, grabbing him and inserting him deeper within her. Her eyes rolled in pleasure, and her mouth filled with saliva. She moved up and down, as if riding a horse, the bed creaking beneath them. A vibration surged through her body from her abdomen, and Neil felt it too. Taking charge, he lifted her, placing her against the wall and thrusting deeper. She dug her nails into his back, moaning softly. A tear lingered at the corner of her eye, signaling her impending climax. Sensing this, he thrust shallowly but faster until she took a deep breath, a mischievous smile spreading across her face. He laid her on the bed, holding her legs up in the air. After a few deep gulps of air, he thrust a few more times, releasing warmth deep inside her. He exhaled, collapsing beside her. She turned to him, pulling him closer, inhaling his natural masculine musk that lingered at the nape of his neck and shoulders.

The girls room was eerily silent, the kind of quiet that makes your skin crawl. Milly sat on her bed, clutching her bracelet, feeling the weight of the night pressing down on her. Shadows danced along the walls, flickering with the faint light from her phone. Each creak of the house seemed louder than the last, echoing her rising anxiety.

Suddenly, a chill swept through the air, and she felt it—a presence lurking just beyond her sight. Heart pounding, she glanced towards the corner, where the darkness seemed to thicken. Was it just her imagination? Or was something really there, watching her?

And then, out of nowhere, a figure emerged from the shadows. The girl stood there, her eyes glinting like sharp knives in the dim light. Milly's breath hitched, her pulse racing as fear gripped her. This wasn't just a figment of her imagination; it was real, and it was terrifying.

"Why are you so scared?" the girl whispered, her voice smooth yet chilling. "I'm not here to hurt you... yet."

Milly wanted to scream, to run, but her body felt frozen, as if the very air around her had turned to ice. "What do you want?" she managed to stammer, her voice barely above a whisper.

The girl took a step closer, a sinister smile creeping across her face. "I want to show you something... something you'll never forget,"

The girl took a step closer, a sinister smile creeping across her face.

Milly's heart raced as the figure stepped out of the shadows, revealing a face that looked exactly like hers but marred with wounds and bruises. "You see, Milly," the girl whispered, her voice dripping with a haunting familiarity, "I'm you... but broken. I'm here to take your soul. No one will believe you when you tell them— they'll just think you're on drugs." Before Milly could process the words, the girl turned and darted toward the broken window pane, shards glinting in the dim light. With a swift motion, she leaped through the glass, disappearing into the night, leaving a chilling silence in her wake.

"Milly!" she heard a voice call from behind her, and she turned to see her sister staring back at her in horror. "You have to listen! I saw it too!"

Chapter 2: Hot pursuit

Samael cautiously followed the blood trails that led into the cave. The creature lurking within knew it was being pursued, and it erupted into a pool of blood, morphing into six distinct shapes that formed six different creatures. The main body was hot on its heels, while the other five did their utmost to hinder Samael's advance. As shadowy figures flanked him, slashing from various angles within the cave, Samael couldn't help but smile at their futile attempts.

What the creatures didn't realize was that Samael was a master of shadow manipulation. He summoned a chain from the darkness, wrapping it around the figures with astonishing speed, despite their frantic movements. Glancing upward, he muttered a few incantations, and the chain ignited in flames, reducing the captured creatures to mere ashes.

Next, he pointed his palm towards the main creature's body, and a chain slithered towards it at an unimaginable velocity. It quickly returned, ensnaring a middle-aged man within its red-hot, twisted links. He was slightly bearded, his eyes blood-red, and he reeked of the salt of blood. Samael locked eyes with him and asked, "Where is Molik?"

"Druf Neizz," it roared, but Samael smacked it across the face and shouted, "English!"

"I don't know; he never reveals his location. He only appears when summoned."

"Lies!" Samael retorted nonchalantly before the chain erupted in flames, turning the man to ashes. Amidst the ashes, he noticed a shiny coin, which he quickly pocketed in a special bag. He then donned the coat he had left on a rock outside, retracted the chains back into the shadows, and stepped out.

He mounted his motorcycle and sped off. As he rode along the road, a dark figure materialized before him prompting him to stop and get off. He genuflected before it and shook its hand before it took off its hoodie, revealing a pale young lady who was probably in her mid ages. "How far are you in capturing Molik?" she asked. "Give me a few more days, and I'll hand him over to the council," he said. "You have one day, or we're deploying Asül." "No, not him, please... ple....!" Before he could finish, she had disappeared into thin air.

Now Asül was the most successful protector in the whole organization. He had protected the whole region for 12 years before Samael was given the position to protect, and Asül was sent to guard over the eastern part of the country. Asül had no remorse whatsoever on demons. To him, they were the reason his mother died, and he never negotiated with them. Now Samael's daughter was partially a demon since he had lain with a demon years back, and the result was the little girl he now cherished and protected with his life. He knew that if Asül was to come to aid in the search for Molik, he would kill every demon in the area, including Lara and Lana (originally Augurs, the demon of the time, and the mother to Lara). Now Lana was badly injured after her last fight with Asül and found refuge in Samael, who hid her in his cellar. The council knew of this, but it was not their concern since to them, their only focus was on Molik (The necromancy demon who had domain over illusions manipulation and brain control). At first,

Molik was harmless until he started finding pleasure in his work and became psychotic and out of control. Asül's return would ensure Molik was dead or captured, but it also would mean death upon Lara and Lana since he knew she was alive and wanted to hunt her down until he was sent to a different location.

Samael thought all this and was deeply troubled. He stood in the middle of the road for what felt like an eternity, grappling with the weight of his thoughts. The looming threat of Asül's return sent shivers down his spine, knowing that it could mean the end for Lara and Lana. The conflict within him intensified as he considered the lives at stake.

Samael took a deep breath, trying to steady his racing heart. He understood the council's obsession with capturing Molik, but the cost of that pursuit was becoming too high. The balance between duty and compassion was tipping dangerously, and he felt the burden of those choices heavy on his shoulders.

Samael took a step back, glancing around as the weight of his thoughts settled in. He knew he had to act fast. With each passing moment, the tension in the air thickened, and the shadows seemed to whisper secrets of what was to come.

Samael made a decision. He would find a way to protect Lara and Lana, even if it meant defying the council. There had to be a way to confront Molik without unleashing Asül's wrath upon them all. Time was running out, and he needed a plan that would save them from the impending doom.

His thoughts were abruptly interrupted by a car honking at him, a reminder that he was standing in the middle of the road. Climbing onto his motorcycle, he sped back home. Upon entering, he found Lara in the living room, absorbed in the television. She was angry with him for trying to reclaim the antique bracelet she had sold—or rather, gifted to her friend.

"Oi! It's rather late; shouldn't you be asleep?" he asked, but she blatantly ignored him.

"Didn't you hear me?" he fumed, struggling to keep his composure. After a moment, he regained control and simply bid her goodnight before heading to the cellar for some wine.

Down there, he found Lana mashing grapes into wine. She looked pale, her veins dark from wounds that had mysteriously begun to reopen.

"Please don't let them summon Asül; I need to see my daughter grow up!" she exclaimed, sensing the fear in his eyes. He moved quickly, catching her in his arms and kissing her forehead.

"Don't worry, no one will take her or you. I will protect you with my life," he reassured her.

Just then, they heard Lara's footsteps stomping away from the living room and up the stairs. Lana paused her mashing, wiped her hands on her apron, and walked out of the cellar and into Lara's room.

———— ◉ ————

"Milly's mental health began to deteriorate as she experienced sudden seizures and convulsions while at school. This deeply concerned her parents. One day in class, a girl sitting next to her tapped her shoulder. When Milly turned around, she witnessed the girl stabbing her own eyes with a pencil multiple times and screaming.

"Don't hurt me, Milly. I just want to be friends with you," the girl cried out.

"Stop screaming! Stop hurting yourself! Please, stop it! You're driving me crazy!" Milly yelled, covering her ears with her palms. The girl paused at these words, gazing at Milly. She then leaned in and whispered, "I will have your soul!" before bursting into laughter, joined by others. Milly covered her ears to drown out the laughter, but then collapsed to the floor, screaming in the middle of the lesson.

Surrounded by concerned classmates trying to comfort her, Milly heard haunting words instead. "You little liar! Your secrets will be exposed!" she heard amidst her cries and rolling on the ground. "Shut up! Be quiet!" she pleaded, as the taunting sounds continued, accusing her of being a lesbian. "It will all come to light soon!" the voices declared before erupting into menacing laughter. As their laughter intensified, their heads began to burst like water balloons, showering blood over her. Milly closed her eyes and screamed, prompting her classmates to restrain her.

"Shut it! Stop it! I'm not a lesbian! I'm straight!" she screamed, still on the floor. Her classmates, confused and alarmed, carried her to the nurse's office, where she was sedated and allowed to rest. Later that afternoon, Molly checked on her and offered to take her home. The principal approved, and Milly went home.

"Can you describe in detail what you witnessed?" Molly demanded during the drive home. Milly was too traumatized to respond; she lay there in silence, her eyes fixed on the road ahead. Upon arriving home, Molly carried her inside and gently placed her on the bed. She then called Milly's mother, who immediately left work and rushed home.

As soon as Mrs. McEwen arrived, Samael knocked on the door. She opened it but quickly tried to close it again, only for him to wedge his foot in the doorway.

"I'm here to save Milly; she needs me," he said softly. Mrs. McEwen sighed and reluctantly let him in. No sooner had he stepped into the girl's room than Milly regained her composure and began to speak clearly. He pulled out two rings and handed them to both Molly and Milly, warning them not to take them off before he left. No one actually saw him go; they just noticed mid-conversation that he was suddenly gone.

The rings were neither flashy nor shabby; they were simple iron bands with inscriptions on the inside that remained a mystery to everyone. Milly then fell back onto the bed, starting to doze off. Her tense demeanor had eased, and for the first time in days, she slept comfortably.

That evening, Neil never returned home; his phone was off, and everyone was worried. Molly called Lara, asking her to relay the news of Neil's disappearance to Samael.

Chapter 3: Asül the terrible

Neil felt utterly exhausted that evening after his shift. He despised being the man behind the computer and wished for his back to heal sooner. In the infantry, he had been one of the best soldiers, quick and precise in his detailed attacks during the war against terrorism. The back injury he sustained from being in the blast zone of a hand grenade had nearly cost him his life. He was fortunate to be alive at that point.

He climbed into his truck and drove home, longing for the scent of his wife's hair as she welcomed him into the house. He craved the warmth of his daughters' embraces as they excitedly recounted their day at school. He sped out of the base and onto the road, eager to return home.

Halfway there, he collided with a speeding deer, which fell onto the asphalt and splattered like a red crayon for several meters before losing momentum and dying. As he stepped out to inspect the scene, he was confronted by the sight of a headless girl lying in the street.

The girl bore a striking resemblance to Milly, sending a chill of fear through him. He turned to grab his coat from the truck, only to come face-to-face with a creature that resembled a deer but had a human body. It seized him by the neck and flung him into the nearby woods as if he were weightless. It then vanished, only to reappear behind him, slamming him against a nearby tree. He had never felt such terror as this creature tossed him around like he weighed nothing at all.

He reached for the strap on his waist and pulled out his revolver, firing at the creature. It fell but quickly sprang back up, gripping him by the neck and pressing his head against the tree in an attempt to crush his skull. Summoning all his strength, he aimed the revolver at the creature's temples and fired the remaining bullets into its head. The creature screamed in agony as it continued to force him against the tree until he lost consciousness.

Suddenly, it tore in half and exploded into a pool of blood. A middle-aged man of slightly heavy build jumped down from the tree above, landing in the blood. He glanced at Neil, who was now slumped against the tree, unconscious. The man hoisted him onto his shoulder and placed him in the car before driving off.

———⟢———

Asül rang the doorbell, and Lana, who was in the cellar reading, quickly transformed into her battle form, a lady with wings made of iron and silver feathers, holding a huge Hourglass. She prepared herself at the door, sensing Asül's presence and ready to fight despite her reopened wounds. Samael, feeling Asül's presence too, directed Lana to her room. He strategically placed the lamp to create multiple shadows around the door and front porch, ready to use them for his chains in case of a fight. When Asül rang the doorbell again, the door opened swiftly. Asül scanned the area, locked eyes with Samael, and simply stated, "wrong house!" After a brief pause, he stormed through the door, knocking Samael to the ground. Samael swiftly summoned a red-hot chain from a shadow cast by the lamp, aiming it at Asül, who agilely dodged, causing the chain to tear through the wall. In retaliation, Samael grabbed the lamp, smashing it onto Asül's head, then, fueled by anger, he wrestled Samael to the ground, readying his dagger for a fatal strike. Before he could stab Samael, Lana threw open the door and unleashed a powerful gust of wind with her wings, knocking Asül off balance and into the wall. Some of her feathers pierced his arm. "Augurs!!!" He yelled, drawing his second dagger and charging at her. She countered with another gust of wind, but he evaded it and hurled a poison dagger at her. Lana shielded herself with her wings, then used her strength to strike him with her wing, showering him with sharp feathers and sending him onto his back. She rushed to Samael, who was concussed on the floor, covering him with her wing. With her other wing, she unleashed a flurry of feathers at Asül, who shielded himself with a couch and his heavy coat.

Lara hurried downstairs to find her injured father on the floor and her mother's true form by his side. Across the room, she saw the burly Asül preparing to attack. "Mom!" she cried out as Asül lunged towards her, causing a distraction. Lana's fist met Asül's knife, shattering it into pieces, but she suffered terrible cuts on her knuckles.

Asül paused his attack and moved to shield Lara, who attempted to fight back. "Stop fighting, I am only trying to rescue you!" he barked.

"NO! You want to kill my parents!" she screamed. The words pierced through his ears, and he halted, looking at both of them on the floor.

Milly opened her eyes to find herself alone in the room. The door to the hall stood ajar, shrouded in darkness. All was pitch black, save for two eyes gleaming from the room across the hallway. She attempted to call out to Molly, but her voice failed her. The eyes drew nearer, revealing a girl with a grievous wound on her neck, moving about the room. Blood cascaded from her neck, staining the floor as she slipped, laughing in a chilling and menacing manner with each fall. She began smearing the blood on her face and delved deep into the wound, retrieving a bloody ring. Milly then realized her own ring was missing.

The creature let out a piercing shriek, dropping to all fours and swiftly advancing towards the bed. Milly struggled, but found herself immobilized. As the creature neared, she felt rooted to the spot. Just as the creature closed in on the bed, Milly, unable to move, observed as the figure vanished into the shadows on the floor. Dismissing it as a nightmare, she turned over, only to come face to face with the girl lying in the adjacent bed. The girl seized her neck, choking her as she fought to break free. Summoning her strength, Milly kicked the girl, propelling her off the bed and into the shadows beneath.

The girl vanished only to reappear at the foot of the bed, yanking Milly off the sheets and into the hallway. She valiantly struggled against the unseen force until Molly emerged from her room, striking the figure squarely on the neck with her guitar, shattering it and causing the creature to dissolve into a pool of blood. Molly then lifted her sister and guided her back to the room. Breathless and frightened, Milly attempted to speak.

"Where is your ring?" Molly inquired urgently. "Your ring! Where is it?" As Milly tried to respond, blood gushed from her mouth, and she collapsed. Alarmed, Molly promptly contacted their mother, who swiftly arrived, carrying Milly in her arms as they rushed to the hospital.

Upon arrival, a few nurses, nearly finishing their shifts, initially scowled but swiftly changed their expressions upon witnessing Milly spitting blood. They acted swiftly, placing her on a gurney and wheeling her into the nearest ward. Startled patients in adjacent beds awoke, screaming in fear. An X-ray revealed a ring lodged deep in her throat. A surgeon was urgently summoned, as waiting until morning would risk severe bleeding. The surgeon acted promptly, extracting the ring. It turned out to be the protective ring gifted by Samael.

Chapter 4: The hunters council

Neil jolted awake, instinctively leveling his revolver at the man behind the wheel. The driver let out a weary sigh, accelerated the car, then abruptly halted, sending Neil sprawling against the glove compartment.

"You're out of bullets, Neil. We'll be there soon," he remarked, glancing down at Neil, whose face was pressed against the cold plastic.

"What happened? Where are you taking me? Where's my car? Who are you?" Neil stammered, fear creeping into his voice as he struggled to regain his composure. The driver shot him a fleeting smile without breaking his gaze from the road. Despite the man's calm demeanor, Neil, a former soldier, sensed an unsettling sincerity beneath the surface.

"Sir, I have a family to get back to," he pleaded, but the driver remained silent, lost in his own thoughts, continuing to drive without a word. Desperate, Neil rifled through his pockets, hoping to find his phone to call home, but it was gone—likely lost in the chaos of his fight with that creature.

Neil vividly recalled everything he had witnessed the previous night. Without a moment's hesitation, he drew his penknife and attempted to stab the silent driver, who was beginning to lose his nonchalant demeanor. Agitated, the driver retaliated, slapping the knife away and sending it tumbling out of the window. Neil struck his chin with his elbow and kicked the driver's thigh, causing the car to veer off the road and crash into a tree. The driver slammed the steering wheel and lay there motionless as Neil crawled out of the vehicle. Although he suspected he had sustained a concussion, he summoned all his strength to flee from the car as quickly as possible.

A branch suddenly fell onto the hood, startling him. He stepped back to check if the driver was still alive, only to discover he had vanished. Turning to escape, he was met with a blow to his face that knocked him unconscious. He collapsed to the ground, and the man hoisted him onto his shoulder, carrying him deeper into the woods. Despite Neil's heavy build, the man lifted him as if he were weightless. They arrived at a cave, where the man placed Neil on the ground and uttered, "arcadis, ardis." In an instant, two men emerged from the thickets, and the man ordered them to carry Neil inside and tend to him.

Neil was awakened by chanting, accompanied by a bright light and some quarrels. He quickly found himself before a council of twelve people—six men and six women. Before the council stood him, the man who had rescued him, and hundreds of other men clad in dark garments. The man who had displayed dominance throughout was now humble; he had removed his hood, revealing a heavily bearded and scarred face, yet he appeared quiet and submissive. Neil wished he could retaliate for the earlier blow.

One of the councilwomen slightly raised her arm, and an ominous silence enveloped the room. Suddenly, it darkened, and she was illuminated by an unknown light.

"Is General Asül amongst us today?" another asked as soon as the room fell silent. Asül, who was in the crowd, stepped forward and glanced back at the people.

"Brothers! As we all know, Molik has broken free and is causing chaos among our towns. We are not safe, as a rat walks amongst us."

He then surveyed the crowd as Princess Augurs was dragged to the front. Her head was covered with a black bag, but her wings and battle armor remained visible and intact.

"We have among us the Time Demon herself, Princess Augurs! Now, as noblemen, we wouldn't kill royal blood, be it human, demon, or deity. However, we must ask Augurs to reveal the identity of the rat, and then we will set her free. It's as simple as that," he smiled.

"I already told you, you sick bastard, I don't have any connection to this. You kidnapped my family and had my husband detained; I will never forgive you for this." Asül smiled, and with a swift backhand, he struck her, sending her crashing to the ground.

"You will talk, and you will talk now!" he grunted. "Bring him out!" he shouted, prompting a few guards to drag the bound Samael onto the podium. A soft, emotional gasp appeared on one of the council members' faces. She frowned and slammed her hand on the table with a thud that silenced everyone in the council; even Asül fell silent. She stood up, joined by all the other council members, and they approached Asül, who quickly genuflected and maintained that position. Samael remained kneeling while Lana, now in her human form, lay on the ground, barely alive.

"We are creatures of light, destined to bring illumination to the world. We are angels and humans; torturing these demons makes us no different from them. From now on, we, as the council, will conduct the interrogation," she growled.
"Permission to speak, your maj..." the lady interrupted sharply.
"Permission not granted!" she snapped, then continued in a much softer tone, "Now, are we clear, General?"
She squatted down, locking eyes with Asül, then touched the back of his robe, scorching it upon contact. The hood disintegrated, leaving him with only his inner cloak.
"Understood!" he replied and vanished so quickly that only the council witnessed his departure. She then gestured to the rest of the crowd, who swiftly carried Samael and Lana into the next room. Neil sat frozen in place until the man who had brought him there lifted him up and walked him outside. He had never encountered such an aura of power and fear.

Back at the hospital, Milly was getting better; she had stopped screaming and was finally eating her meals without help. Molly had never left her side; even late at night, she would crawl into bed, sleep next to her, and cuddle her close. Mrs. McEwen continuously searched for Neil but never found him. She eventually resorted to going to Samael's residence, where she found the house ransacked and in disarray. A few hours later, she received a call from the police department. They had found Neil's car, but no one was in it; it was carefully parked in the middle of the road, in the middle of nowhere. There were no traces of Neil, but signs of a struggle—blood smeared on the trees beside the road.

When the news reached Molly, her heart shattered, but she kept her composure; she didn't want to tell Milly. Both she and her mother believed that revealing the truth would hinder Milly's healing process. Instead, they lied to her, saying Neil was stuck at the office that night and was very busy. They promised her he would visit as soon as she healed. Milly was young but not naive; she sensed something was off, yet she didn't want to worry them, so she kept her cool and pretended to believe them. That night, as she slept, Molly cuddled close, wrapping her tightly. She liked the warmth. Suddenly, the embrace loosened, and before she knew it, Molly was out of bed. As Milly rolled over to look, she saw her. Molly stood there, quiet and stiff as a board. Her arms were dusty, as if she had been digging in the dirt. In her hand, she held her father's head. Maggots and centipedes crawled from the eye sockets of the head she clutched, and it drooled. Her father's head opened its mouth and said, "I'm sorry."
Molly then raised the severed head to her face and pressed her lips against it passionately. As she pulled away from the kiss, she clamped its tongue between her teeth. With tremendous force, she smashed the head onto the ground, where it erupted into a grotesque explosion of decayed, maggot-ridden flesh. Milly recoiled, feeling a wave of nausea wash over her. Just then, Molly emerged from the bathroom doorway, locking eyes with her malevolent doppelgänger. The doppelgänger smirked, and as it turned to face Mrs. McEwen, who attempted to strike it but missed, the creature passed through her like a wraith and vanished. It reappeared behind Molly, and before Milly could issue a warning, it seized her and dragged her into the bathroom, slamming the door shut.

Milly struggled to rise from her bed, but her mother restrained her. She rushed to the bathroom door, but it was jammed and resistant to her efforts. She screamed for assistance, but no sound emerged. The room darkened, and its walls became fluid and undulating. Milly sank deeper into her bed as her mother grappled to pull her out, only to be drawn in further. The screams emanating from the bathroom intensified, leaving Mrs. McEwen torn between whom to assist. Suddenly, the ground beneath her transformed into liquid, and hands reached up to ensnare her. As she began to sink, a chain burst through the door, coiling around her and yanking her from the fluid, incinerating the sinister hands in the process.

The figure behind the chains was Samael. As soon as he set her aside, he sent another chain through the bathroom door, shattering it into fragments. He plunged inside, retrieved the weary Molly, and carried her out. He was too late to save Milly, who had vanished entirely into the sheets. He dispatched his chain after her, but the portal sealed shut, causing the chain to obliterate the bed instead. Mrs. McEwen enveloped Molly in her arms, watching helplessly as the room returned to normalcy without Milly present. Samael then grasped both their shoulders and declared, "It is no longer safe here; follow me!"

"But what about my daughter?" she pleaded.

"She is no longer here, but where we are heading, we stand a better chance of locating her. Now, let us depart," he insisted, striding away with urgency. The two women stood paralyzed, gazing at the bed, before finally turning and sprinting after Samael, who was already halfway down the corridor.

Chapter 5: Molik's Domain

The council reached an agreement that Asül would lead a seven-man army to the mountains to seal the demon portal. He was also tasked with eliminating anyone in the area who had participated in the opening ritual. On his team, he had six of the most elite hunters. Samael was originally meant to be part of this expedition, but after witnessing his ongoing conflict with Asül, it was deemed safer to assign them to separate missions. Samael, on the other hand, was to track down Molik with the assistance of Augurs, while Lara was held captive in case they strayed from the mission. Since Milly was the one Molik desired, they needed to locate her first.

Milly's voice echoed as she screamed at the top of her lungs. She called for Molly and her mother, but no one was around. She found herself trapped in a void room where the lights flickered on and off every fifteen seconds. Whenever the lights went out, she was transported to a realm of pure nostalgia and melancholy.

After the first fifteen seconds, she found herself in the hospital where she was born. She wandered around and saw a four-year-old Molly, brimming with excitement as she begged her mother to let her hold the baby. On the opposite side of the hospital bed stood Neil. He looked genuinely happy; in fact, it was the happiest she had ever seen him. He was quite young, but smile lines creased his face. As she looked closer, she noticed a tall figure lurking behind Neil, watching as the family celebrated the child. The figure then reached out its hands toward the baby, who giggled and raised her arms in response. In a panic, she shouted at the child to stop, triggering a reaction from everyone in the room.

"No one had noticed her presence until they all turned towards her. The seven-foot-tall figure swiftly stabbed Neil at his right temple with a long dagger. He fell without a sound, blood streaming from his eyes and mouth. The rest of the family, gripped by madness, tore the baby apart limb by limb, their laughter echoing like deranged maniacs while she screamed in agony. As they finished the gruesome act, they advanced towards Milly, who desperately tried to intervene.

She managed to evade her 'father's' grasp and her mother's embrace, fleeing to safety. Racing down the hallway, she stumbled over an obstacle. Looking back, she saw Molly, blood oozing from her mouth, but her eyes remained clear. Despite Molly's pleas not to run, the menacing figures closing in on her compelled Milly to break free and escape. Pushing through the hospital's main door, darkness enveloped her, transporting her back to the initial room.

Struggling to catch her breath, she leaned against the wall, leaving bloody handprints as she crawled away, leaving a trail of blood behind. The flickering light caught her attention, and as she opened her eyes, she found herself in Lara's room. Hidden inside the wardrobe, she observed Lara undressing, preparing for a shower. Since the age of 12, Milly had harbored forbidden desires for Lara, considering her the most alluring girl in school.

She watched as Lara's dress gracefully slid down her slender waist and curvaceous hips, feeling an intense longing for her. The visitor was her, but a year younger. She watched as her Doppelgänger embraced Lara, kissing her neck, leaving her breathless. Pulling back Lara's hair, she revealed her lush neck, kissing and caressing it with her nose. Lara pushed her onto the bed, dropping her towel to expose her succulent waist and pale posterior. Climbing on top, she kissed her passionately and deeply. Soft moans escaped her as she gently rubbed Lara's genitals.

Inside the wardrobe, Milly felt a rush of arousal, letting out soft moans as she experienced the moment. It was her first time making love to anyone, especially a woman, and the memories ran deep. Suddenly, she stepped on the wardrobe's ledge, causing the door to swing open. The two lovers on the bed turned towards the wardrobe. Milly's doppelgänger approached Lara with a penknife, while Lara grabbed her softball bat from under the bed, advancing towards her. As Lara flung the door open, Milly jumped out, screaming and pleading for mercy. Lara swung her bat, hitting Milly's shoulder, before the doppelgänger Milly stabbed her in the eye, causing her to halt. Removing the penknife from Lara's eye, it came out with the eye. Milly screamed in agony as the doppelgänger turned towards her, ready to strike before vanishing.

The lights flickered once more, and she found herself back in the initial room. This time, she noticed the walls closing in on her from both sides. Running towards one of the walls, she pushed it back. With another flicker of the lights, she was suddenly in the woods. Recognizing the place from her camping trip at age 12, she hid behind a tree, waiting for any signs of movement. She was wary of encountering the doppelgängers. She crept slowly behind the trees, hiding from the group of students passing by. Among them, she spotted her younger self joyfully skipping with her classmates. They ascended the mountain, eventually setting up camp 500 meters from the summit. While everyone busied themselves with pitching tents, the boys playfully hurled sticks at each other. Spotting a group of students heading her way, she swiftly scaled a tree for cover. Witnessing two boys chasing little Milly, she realized her younger self was unaware of their true intentions. As they led her deeper into the forest, away from the campsite, they pinned her down and assaulted her. A wave of trauma washed over her as she witnessed the events unfold, feeling the pain as her doppelgänger was violated. Descending the tree, she intervened, knowing the consequences if she didn't. In a swift move, she tackled the boys, sending them tumbling downhill and crashing into trees. Rushing to the semi-conscious little Milly, blood seeping from beneath her skirt, she helped her to her feet. As little Milly shrieked, "Bear!" in panic, Molly hurled a rock at her, and soon the tour guide arrived with a shotgun. Little Milly questioned why tranquilizer darts weren't used, but Molly silenced her. They watched as the tour guide fired, the shot piercing through the bear's, the real Milly's, right rib, causing it to collapse.

They huddled up and started walking back to the camp. As she lay there, missing her entire right rib, the dark figure from the hospital ordeal in the first scene appeared and began dragging her by the foot uphill. She was too weak and injured to fight back, only able to watch as she was dragged like a carcass. While being pulled uphill, she caught a glimpse of Little Milly, who was being covered up. Milly was too traumatized to speak, and the boys claimed that the bear had attacked her, not them. Milly's eyes slowly shut, and when the light returned, she found herself back in the room, uninjured but with aching ribs and crotch. She lay there motionless for a few minutes.

———◉———

General Asül's arrival at the mountain was met with strong retaliation. He had never faced such fierce resistance as he did with Kai, the probability demon and the most powerful prince among the seven.

"Asül, I was waiting for you," said Kai as he glided down from the summit of the mountain. He was of average height, but when he shape-shifted into his battle form, he grew to 6'3". His left arm transformed into bronze, while his right arm held a brass scale. His hair was blonde, and his eyes glowed red. His breastplate, made of iron, radiated a red-hot glow.

Asül felt the earth tremble under Kai's enormous power. He couldn't show his fear, but Kai sensed it. Kai wasn't foolish; he knew what skills Asül possessed. Taking down his sister proved Asül's strength. Asül's men surrounded him, but he commanded them to stop. Kai didn't come alone; he had his minions with him, deploying 450 of them with a flick of his hand.

The minions, all clad in black, moved fast toward the expedition, and Asül quickly deployed his men. The battle was fierce, adrenaline pumping through him as he ripped off the heads of at least 20 minions. But then, he caught sight of Kai sitting beside a tree, a sinister smile creeping across his face.

Kai picked up a rock, his eyes calculating the probability and trajectory, knowing it could shift the battle's tide. Mustering all his strength, he hurled the rock toward Asül, who dodged it effortlessly. But it caught one of his men in the lower arm, ripping it clean off. A collective gasp echoed through the air, the horror of that power sinking in.

"Huddle up!" Asül yelled, urgency lacing his voice. His men quickly huddled behind him, fear mingling with determination as they devised a new strategy. Asül felt a surge of protectiveness for his men, knowing their lives depended on his next move. More minions flowed out from the summit of the mountain, and he held them off with every ounce of speed he had while they planned.

The atmosphere was heavy with an unsettling tension as the shadows lengthened around them. Asül, heart pounding, surveyed the desolate landscape, where remnants of past battles lay scattered like forgotten dreams. Every rustle of the leaves seemed to whisper secrets of the lurking dangers, heightening his sense of foreboding. He could feel the weight of his companions' gazes, their expressions a mix of fear and determination, as they prepared to face the impending confrontation.

Suddenly, a chilling howl pierced the silence, echoing through the trees like a harbinger of doom. The ground trembled beneath their feet, a palpable reminder of the dark forces gathering to challenge them. Asül tightened his grip on his weapon, adrenaline coursing through his veins. He knew that the time for hesitation had passed; they had to act swiftly or risk being consumed by the encroaching darkness.

With a fierce resolve, Asül led his comrades forward, each step a testament to their unwavering courage. The path ahead was fraught with peril, yet they pressed on, united in their quest to vanquish the malevolent presence that threatened their existence. Asül's mind raced with strategies, his instincts honed by countless encounters with the sinister forces that sought to destroy them. He understood that victory would demand not only strength but also cunning and unity.

Kai, sensing the shift, stood up and hovered toward the fight, his eyes locked on Asül. The tension thickened as the stakes rose higher—this was a battle they couldn't afford to lose.

Chapter 6: Melancholic nostalgia

Milly lay on the floor, staring at the ceiling. It had been 15 minutes, and she hadn't changed her surroundings. She was finally at peace, unaware that she was lying on her 'bed back at home.' Neil entered the room, followed closely by Molly, with Lara trailing a few seconds later. When they saw Milly on the bed, they all rushed toward her.

"We thought we lost you," Lara said tearfully, extending her hand to Milly, who struggled to move due to her injuries. When their hands touched, they held each other tightly. Suddenly, the room was engulfed in an ominous silence. When the light returned, Milly found herself in a mass grave, still holding Lara's hand. She was pale, lying there with a massive laceration on her shoulder and neck. At the opening of the grave, Aunt Gladys stood with a spade, pouring dirt over Milly and the other bodies, no matter how loudly she screamed.

Molly then appeared behind her and pushed her into the grave. Milly fell onto Lara's body, crushing it under her weight. Lara's corpse expelled blood due to the heavy woman who had fallen directly onto her chest.

"Milly, hold my hand!" shouted Molly, stretching out her hand to pull Milly out of the grave. Aunt Gladys, whose neck had been dislocated by the fall, snapped back to her senses and grabbed Molly's hand, pulling her into the grave as well. As she fell, everything went dark.

When Milly opened her eyes, she was in her childhood kindergarten class. She was seated in the second-to-last row at the back, happily singing the alphabet. The teacher walked slowly toward her and tapped her shoulder. The tap felt real, and for a moment, Milly thought she was back in reality, that all of this had just been a bad dream.

"Milly dear, we are singing the numbers song, not the alphabet song," she said in a soft voice that brought Milly back to her senses. The whole class burst into an uproarious laughter, turning her red with embarrassment. Just then, her deskmate called her close and whispered in her ear, "You're nothing but a dumb bitch!" he said in a sinister voice, and the whole class cackled even more menacingly. "Try to keep up or the wolves will get you!" As she turned to answer him back, she noticed she was alone in the class. At the front, the teacher stood with two boys who knelt with their heads down.

"Milly honey, you decide their fate," she said calmly, smiling. Just as Milly opened her mouth to speak, she interrupted, "before you speak, I'll show you their faces," she said, smiling. She held up one of the boys' faces to reveal Jake, and the other one was obviously Luke, the two boys who raped her on the mountain when she was 12. Seeing that, she sat back down and said no word. Her teacher pulled down two ropes from the class ceiling and put them around the boys' necks. Milly was still quiet, not blinking, just watching as blood started flowing from her crotch, unaware of it. The teacher then pulled the ropes up, looking at Milly in the eyes as they watched the two boys kick and fight for their lives. She then released them, and they fell to the ground gasping for air as she shouted in a deep, rusty masculine voice, "You hateful little girl, your heart is dark and rotten with hatred, a perfect habitat," she screamed.

Just then, Neil walked into the classroom. The teacher kept quiet and stopped in her tracks. He looked at Milly. "Come, we are going home," he said, smiling. Milly didn't argue; she agreed and followed his father as he held her.

"You should not be self-willed, my darling; it kills modesty," Neil said, breaking the silence as they walked past the bathrooms. She looked up at her father, wanting to respond, but her gaze fell on his face, half-eaten like a bun, his skin pale as that of a corpse. She quickly screamed, breaking free from his grip and running all the way to the bathroom.

"You can't run far, darling. You leave behind a trail of hatred and vengeance. Your bloodlust burns bright, even if you hide in the dark," he called after her.

"You are not my dad! Stay away from me!" she shouted, locking the bathroom door behind her and bolting it shut.

"You reek of hatred. I will catch you! I will dismember you piece by piece, and I will take your dark, twisted soul. I LOVE IT WHEN YOU RUN!" he shouted, banging on the door. She braced herself against it, trying to prevent Evil Neil from breaking in. Just then, she heard sticky footsteps from inside one of the bathroom stalls. Fear rooted her to the spot. Aunty Gladys emerged from the bathroom, barefoot, leaving behind a trail of bloody footprints.

"You left me to die on that mountain! I hope you die!" she spat, before blindly running into one of the sinks, crashing into it, shattering the mirror, and collapsing in a pool of blood pooling from her head.

In that moment, Evil Neil broke down the door and rushed in, grabbing Milly by her foot and lifting her into the air. Aunty Gladys, bleeding and clutching her arms, pulled Milly in the opposite direction. Milly felt her spine detach, and at that moment, she accepted death.

"You won't get far! I told you that!" Evil Neil taunted. Aunty Gladys laughed maniacally as she pulled harder. Milly screamed, feeling her knees and elbows beginning to crack out of their joints. This was a painful way to die. "If only Molly were here; she always knew what to do," she thought to herself.

———◆———

"I see bubbles!" Molly shouted as she plunged her whole body into the bog. She felt a soft, warm form and was sure it was Milly. With hands gripping the body beneath the water, she struggled before finally freeing her. She pulled Milly out, who appeared half-conscious, and began to tread carefully through the bog to join Samael and her mother, who were on the other side of the river.

Milly's body was covered in bruises, scratches, a deep neck laceration, and broken ribs. As Molly placed her into Samael's arms, Milly moaned in pain but didn't regain consciousness. She cried out, "Forgive me, Aunty Gladys! I didn't mean for this to happen. I'm not hateful! Please don't break my back, Dad!" All the while, she struggled against invisible chains.

Samael wrapped her in his chains and laid her on the ground.

He then instructed the two women to step back about 100 meters. "Don't come any closer, no matter what. I can't save you once I start the ritual."

They couldn't argue, as they all trusted him; he had saved them twice before. Gradually, they took steps back as he urged them to move. Once they were far enough away, he gave them a thumbs up.

He took a deep breath, and his eyes slowly turned pale. Milly began to scream in agony, igniting Mrs. McEwen's maternal instincts. She asked Samael if Milly was alright, but he remained silent. She wanted to rush to him, but Molly held her back. "Mom, remember the rules—don't go any closer!" she urged. "But they're hurting Milly!" her mother shouted back. As she tried to step forward, she watched in awe as Samael began to levitate slowly in the air. Milly became rigid, and she too lifted off the ground, her screams echoing through the dark woods. Mrs. McEwen couldn't hold back any longer; she dashed forward just as Samael was about to complete the ritual.

In an instant, both Milly and Samael plummeted back down, and the nearest tree began to splinter apart. A powerful force erupted, sending them all flying to the far end of the clearing. Milly crashed into Molly and her mother, while Samael quickly secured his chain around a sturdy tree branch, regaining his balance. He hurled his chain toward the tree, which was being violently torn asunder by opposing forces.

The chain blazed a fiery red as it sliced through the tree, finally coming to a halt as everything returned to an eerie calm. Samael glared down at Mrs. McEwen, who lay sprawled on the ground. "If it weren't for sheer luck, you would've been the one ripped in half. I transferred the force from your daughter onto that tree; I had no idea it would be so powerful. You're just lucky it didn't tear you apart."

They then shifted their focus to Milly, who appeared relaxed yet still unconscious. Without wasting a moment, they rushed her to the base; the councilmen were definitely going to want a word with her. She was their only connection to Molik's discovery.

Chapter 7: Battle Royale

Back at the battlegrounds, Asül suffered great losses. One of his men was overwhelmed and dismembered, while two others were chewed up alive. The last man, whose hand had been ripped clean off, collapsed due to blood loss. Asül exhausted all his skills and weaponry to fight Kai, but unlike the Augurs, Kai was faster—almost as fast as Asül himself. His thick iron armor rendered physical attacks nearly useless. Even after killing all of Kai's minions, the elite force was still no match.

Using a crafty technique to reduce the probability of his opponents' victory, he scattered them in different directions, making them weaker. If Asül hadn't been part of the battle, they would have lost by now. His power gave him an above-average win probability despite all of Kai's antics. The probability deduction technique worked better on weaker fighters; Asül had a 70% win probability, but despite his efforts, Kai's technique reduced it all the way down to 48%.

Asül moved swiftly and cut off Kai's right arm. Kai stood motionless for a few seconds before looking up at Asül and smiling menacingly. "You are mine!" he shouted, charging toward Asül while quickly regenerating his hand. The other men attacked but were thrown far from the battlefield by an unknown force. Asül stood still as the demon rushed at him, and when he saw an opening to land a fatal blow, he moved gracefully, as if dancing with the air. He grabbed the demon's left arm and ripped it clean off at the shoulder. Using it as a club, he knocked Kai away, sending him flying through the air. Kai laughed even harder as he crashed into trees, breaking them apart. Asül charged toward him at lightning speed, slamming him into the trees harder than before.

Kai's laughter only agitated Asül further, prompting him to strike continuously. As if rejuvenated with newfound strength, Kai regenerated his hands and used them to propel himself away from Asül's punches. He then snatched Asül's dagger and plunged it deep into his shoulder.

"Curse you, Kai!" Asül groaned in pain. "I will make you pay for this!"

"Poor human," Kai taunted. "You can't defeat me. I've slain angels in battle, and you are barely a match for me!"

"I am General Asül, and by my hand, the entire demon race will fall!" Asül declared sternly.

"You are strong, but you're just a man..." Kai's words were abruptly cut short as one of Asül's men stabbed him in the shoulder. Enraged, he seized the man by the neck, locking eyes with him as he slowly crushed his throat. Another assailant lunged at him, only to have his head cleanly severed when Kai swung his hand.

Asül sobbed silently, summoning all his strength. He yanked Kai's hair and struck him back fiercely with his heels, nearly tearing through to his chest. Kai groaned in pain and retaliated by lifting Asül by the neck and hurling him like a discus into a tree. As he charged forward, a heavy gunshot rang out, sending him crashing to the ground. Neil emerged from behind a tree, firing multiple shots at Kai before Asül stopped him.

"That won't work on him!" Asül shouted, swinging his dagger as he lunged toward Kai. He slashed at Kai, who had just regained his footing, cutting deeply into his chest.

As Kai screamed in agony, Neil continued to fire at him. Caught off guard, Kai felt the last swing of Asül's dagger sever his hands at the wrists. A man appeared from behind and thrust a javelin through the back of Kai's head, the tip emerging from his eye. They watched as he collapsed to the ground.

As the man rushed to help Asül up, Kai, despite his injuries, seized the javelin and hurled it at him, ripping through his back, causing him to fall. He approached Asül, who, though wounded, still possessed enough strength to fend him off. "You're powerful for a human, but after all, you're just human," he said with disgust. "I don't care if you're invincible or invulnerable; you will die by my hand!" Asül tightened his grip on his dagger, took a deep breath, and sprinted at Kai, who charged back at him with equal speed. Kai hardened his skin and grew two sharp, knife-like protrusions from his arms. He hurled them at Asül, who sliced cleanly through them. As soon as Kai was close enough, he kicked at him, but Asül caught his foot, swept him off his other leg, and drove his knee into Kai's face. He then hurled him into the air, and Kai crashed against a tree. A branch tore through the back of his shoulder as Asül yanked him by the leg, ripping his shoulder bone out of its socket.

Although Kai was supposed to scream in pain, he burst into loud laughter. "Meredith!" he shouted, causing Asül to halt in his tracks. He continued, "She cried for her life as I gouged her eyes out." This enraged Asül further, and he mounted Kai, sitting on his chest, and began to punch his skull with ferocity.

"No! Don't kill me; I have a son!" he mimicked Meredith's voice, further infuriating Asül. He continued to laugh mockingly as heavy blows landed on his face, reducing his head to a mush. Slowly, he transformed back into his human form. Just as Asül was about to deliver one final, crushing blow, a familiar heavy voice cut through the air, bringing everything to a halt.

"That will be all, General; we need him to escort us!" said one of the council members who had arrived at the scene. She spread her arms and split into twelve different figures. Everyone present quickly bowed, and Kai began to regenerate. As they were about to bow before the council, Kai seized the moment and fled the scene. He wasn't supposed to run, but no one dares to mess with the council of deities.

The council men merged into one and opened a void, running quickly into it, appearing before Kai. Kai bumped into them but they didn't budge. They stood before him and split into 12 men who surrounded Kai. He wielded fire from hell and tried to burn the council in confusion as he fled, but the fire didn't harm them. They all asked in unison, "Will you accompany us and answer some questions?"

Kai grabbed a chunk of earth and threw it at a council member, but the member stopped it with his palm and disintegrated it. Feeling trapped, Asül poured his blood onto the ground and summoned all the demon royalty, causing a great tremor. The royal demons disappeared and reappeared near the council. The councilmen merged into one main body and floated over the sky. The royal demons bowed before the council, not daring to challenge them. The council spoke with a heavy voice, making the area windy and shaky. When a royal demon tried to speak, a thin sheet of air decapitated him.

"You will speak when spoken to, Creature of the dark!" they roared. "For 700 years, we've maintained balance across the realm, and you demons are ruining everything. Molik roams among us, and none of you royals are doing anything about it. We sent our task force to discuss this, and you have murdered them all. Don't force our hand, or we will ensure the end of the demon race. Capture Molik and bring him to us if you know what's good for you. Failure to comply will result in the entire realm being reduced to ashes."

With a deafening roar, they vanished into a blinding beam of light that nearly blinded all the humans in the area. The royal demons understood that fighting the humans was futile at that moment, so they sank back into the shadows of the ground. Asül lay against a tree, panting as he tried to heal himself. Neil knelt beside him, offering support. At that moment, one of the injured men from Asül's task force stirred slightly, breathing softly. No one noticed him. He rolled onto his back, taking a silent breath. Once the area was cleared and the bodies removed, he opened his eyes and gazed up at the sky. He felt cold and numb; he couldn't feel his arm, partly because it had been severed. In the darkest part of the mountain, he spotted a few shadowy figures gathering. Quickly, he rolled into a bush, covering his injured arm with his hood, and silently waited as seven other demons began to converse.

"We don't have the upper hand; let's surrender Molik, and everything will be alright!" said the first demon.

"We possess two of the Earth's orbs; Kai has the third. With all four, we can banish the deities from the human realm," replied another demon.

"What if the deities beat us to it? Huh, there's no way out of that!" the first demon replied, agitation creeping into his voice.
"What if they don't?" countered another demon, his tone surprisingly optimistic. "Be positive for once."
"I'm a damn demon! Positivity isn't in my nature, you fool!"
"Is it any wonder you're the weakest among us?"
"Don't test me, you fool. Don't you dare!"
Just as the tension peaked and the two demons seemed ready to clash, Genta, the matter demon who had taken Augur's place after her presumed death, stepped in between them. Kai raised his hand, and an uneasy silence fell over the group.
"Listen up!" he commanded, his voice steady. "The deities have always held the upper hand, but we're done with it. We must expel them from this world, and that's final. And—" he paused, sniffing the air, "there's a human nearby."
With that, Genta unleashed a fireball towards the bush, flames roaring as they consumed everything in their path, revealing an injured man crouched within the flames. The demons turned in unison, their eyes glinting with malice as they charged forward, a wave of chaos and hunger.

Chapter 8: Locked out of the sky

The injured man knew he was done for. He could try outrunning the demons, but he wouldn't get far. Fighting them was also an option, but with one arm, he knew he stood no chance against even a single one. If he didn't escape, the demons would kill him in the most excruciating way possible.

On the other hand, the demons were aware that he would reveal the secrets he had overheard if set free. As they charged at him, Genta hurled a fireball in his direction. Thinking quickly, he dodged it, knowing he wasn't strong enough to return it given the immense power it held.

Taking short, deep breaths that quickened his heart rate, he propelled himself away from the charred bush with one great leap. His arm had stopped bleeding, but he left behind a trail of fear. He hastened his steps, weaving between the trees at a tremendous speed. Rocks were hurled at him like bullets from a machine gun, but he was quick enough to dodge them all. Adrenaline coursed through his veins; it was either he escaped or he died. As he ran downhill, Kai signaled to the other demons to quickly surround him. They were fast, but no one could catch up to him just yet. Genta flew past him, creating a heavy gust of wind in an attempt to stop him, but he maneuvered through the breeze, making his body as aerodynamic as possible. He slipped through Genta's wind slice, but it caught his hood, ripping it off his body.

The air was thick with tension as the demons drew closer, their guttural growls echoing through the shadows. With 17 years of grueling training behind him, he was ready to unleash his skills. He executed the super jump, a maneuver perfected to propel anyone—regardless of weight—at least 700 feet into the air, ensuring a flawless landing. A single miscalculation could shatter his femur. He inhaled deeply mid-jump, channeling a surge of blood into his calves, and launched himself upward with such ferocity that the ground beneath him fractured under the strain. A wave of relief washed over him as he realized it had worked.

As he descended, he quickly scanned his surroundings, landing at the mountain's base before sprinting away. Though the jump had drained much of his strength, he pressed on. Suddenly, he spotted Samael, navigating the mountain's foot with Milly draped over his shoulder, while Molly and Mrs. McEwen followed closely behind, accompanied by a few other hunters. Samael recognized the urgency in his eyes and sprang into action, swiftly instructing three of his men to escort Milly, Molly, and Mrs. McEwen to safety.

The powerful demons were closing in, their strength rivaling that of his wife—perhaps even surpassing it. Ears, one of his men, felt the ground tremble beneath the weight of the approaching beasts, estimating they were a mere 50 seconds away. Time was not on their side. They couldn't flee with Milly, Molly, and Mrs. McEwen, who were no match for the speed of the seasoned hunters. The injured hunter was ordered to escape, as he was the primary target. Samael and six of his elite soldiers would remain behind to confront the impending onslaught, fully aware that this battle was one they could not win. They had instructed the remaining hunters to call for reinforcements as soon as they reached safety.

As night enveloped the battlefield, Samael felt a surge of advantage coursing through him. The hellfire chains, his weapon of choice, flickered ominously in the darkness, ready to strike from every direction. He steeled himself, knowing that the deities would soon arrive to turn the tide. Counting down the seconds, he felt his heart race with fear, but he pushed it aside; the demons could smell fear, and he wouldn't give them the satisfaction.

Suddenly, Kai and Genta swooped in, their arrival swift and unexpected. Genta unleashed a powerful gust of wind that sent the men staggering, caught off guard. In an instant, Samael summoned his chains, igniting them with hellfire as they shot toward the demons, who scattered in panic. He gestured urgently to his men, signaling them to spread out, becoming harder targets in the chaos.

But just as they began to run, the rest of the demon royalty emerged, their presence suffocating. Their power radiated, nearly rivaling that of the deities, and Samael felt it like a weight on his chest. The deities had the advantage of speed, coordination, and the terrifying ability to disintegrate matter itself. Their swiftness was unmatched, and Samael's thoughts drifted to Asül; if only he were here, the odds might shift in their favor.

He didn't need to win the battle—he just had to hold on until the cavalry arrived. But time was slipping away. One of the demons, desperate and clumsy, stumbled upon the emerald orb—the last piece they needed to banish the deities from the earth. The stakes were higher than ever; they had to decide—kill the hunters first and risk the ritual's failure, or perform the ritual before the hunters were eliminated, all while knowing the deities could interrupt at any moment.

They quickly pounced on the hunters, and Samael, quick and keen, drove his chain through Genta, sending him flying a few meters away. He was scorched and knew it would take a few minutes to regenerate. At that moment, Kai sank into a shadow and appeared behind Samael, grabbing his neck and choking him. He summoned all the hell fires onto Samael, aiming to burn him to a crisp. But Samael, a wielder of fiery techniques, quickly deflected the attack back at Genta, interrupting his healing process.

The other five demons split themselves; two pursued the fleeing hunters while the other two began the ritual. One of them, Kraus, the demon with command over the underworld, joined Kai and Genta in battling Samael and his team. The clash was fierce, with both sides matched in combat. As the night deepened, the demons grew stronger, their dark powers swelling in the shadows. By midnight, they would fuse into the powerful and invincible demon king.

❦

"The demons, they're... they're plotting, Mount Russ..." the man gasped before collapsing before the council. The council quickly deployed 72 of the highest-ranking hunters. Asül was meant to join but was nursing his injuries. The hunters sprinted toward the mountain, where vehicles couldn't easily reach. Along the way, they encountered the twin earth demons, who, upon seeing the large number of hunters, quickly turned and fled back to the mountain.

Upon arrival, they found three dead men, victims of the demons. Genta was half-dead, Samael having burned his head before he could heal. The ritual was just two minutes from completion, and the demons descended upon the newly arrived hunters. Shaka sunk his fingers into the ground, causing the earth twins to crack the surface. Many low-ranking demons surged from the earth, charging at the hunters. But the hunters, fierce and skilled, tore through them with ease, cutting them down quicker than they arrived. Samael wielded his chains, slicing through hordes of demons.

Just as they were about to finish the ritual, the council members arrived from the sky, merging into a single entity that disintegrated the demon hordes upon contact. As they drew close to Kai, they seized him and flung him into the air, the acrid smell of burnt flesh and the echoes of battle cries filling the night, mingling with the crackling of flames.

THE END

―――――●―――――

Teaser for Invincible: The Grave Robber volume 2

As the council members approached the ritual grounds to halt the ominous ceremony, an unseen force yanked them back, causing them to collapse onto the earth. Desperately, they attempted to rise, transforming into their battle forms—a powerful, winged male—but an icy grip seized them, rendering them immobile. Though their breaths came in shallow gasps, they remained rooted to the ground, slowly morphing into silver statues, their hands raised toward the darkening sky. Those nearby could sense their once-mighty power trapped in a single point, gradually dissipating into the chilling air....

Don't miss out!

Visit the website below and you can sign up to receive emails whenever Luke Pens publishes a new book. There's no charge and no obligation.

https://books2read.com/r/B-A-RGDYC-MYUJF

BOOKS 2 READ

Connecting independent readers to independent writers.

Also by Luke Pens

Invincible
Invincible: The Grave Robber
Invincible: The Grave Robber ; Vol 2

About the Author

Beevan(Bevan) Lucky alias Luke Pens started writing at a fairly young age of 14 years and has written for 6 years so far, while he may fall back as an author new to the game , he is definitely good at what he does. He lives in Kenya with his family and likes drawing, playing basketball, video editing and reading historical books. Despite constantly working on Horror, thriller and fantasy books he is currently working on a new romance book alongside Invincible:The Grave Robber Vol 3. He drives inspiration from Stephen King, J.K Rowling, Shayla black and Fyodor Dostoevsky.